A Little Queermas Carol

***

SASSAFRAS LOWREY

Published in 2016 by PoMo Freakshow Press
Brooklyn, New York USA
www.PoMoFreakshow.com

Copyright © 2016 Sassafras Lowrey
Printed in the United States of America
ISBN: 978-0-9857009-1-1

Cover design: KD Diamond
Copy Editing: Gabrielle Harbowy
Book Design: Jacob Tavares

＊＊＊

For all the littles who have
(re)discovered/(re)claimed the magic of Christmas
& for the Bigs who bring the season
to life for us.

Introduction:

The ghosts you are about to meet are real and trauma, imagination, and faith. They appear as both visions and flashbacks...

Part 1:
Marley

ometimes there is nothing to do but commit to being miserable. It's like when your stockings lose their elastic and you are walking down the street and they start slipping down your thighs, and then when they get to your knees you convince yourself it's a look and keep walking, and then they slip and sit baggy around your shins, and there is no appropriate way to hike them back up to your crotch so you just let them sag, hold your head high, and walk on in misery. Life was often like that for Ebe. Especially since Marley was dead.

It had been seven months, but to Ebe it felt like seven minutes since they learned that Marley was gone. They had done everything together, except this, though sometimes Ebe wished more than anything this was something they could share. It almost didn't feel worth being alive without Marley. Ebe had such a hard time figuring out what they wanted or connecting with anyone. Marley made them a better person at least in their friendship. It was the two of them against the world, they were living queer feminist anti-racist vegan anarchist anti-capitalist environmentalist righteous lives and were going to bring about the revolution together. Without hir there didn't seem much point to anything, but Ebe knew Marley would kick their ass if they followed in hir footsteps.

One of the hardest things about Marley being gone was not knowing what had happened. The police said it was it was suicide, but that's what everyone thinks when someone dies. I guess that's what it means to be young and queer, everyone just fucking walking around terrified about who in the community is going to do it next. It's a fucked up way to live, panicking whenever your phone rings because it might be the phone tree letting you know another friend is dead so you don't find out on the Internet or in a text message. Maybe it's not just a queer thing, maybe this is what the whole world is like right now. Ebe didn't know. All they knew was that this is what their world had become. Ebe had known Marley better than anyone and they just couldn't believe Marley would have done it, at least not intentionally. Shit must have gotten really out of hand. Ze'd been clean and things had been so much better, Ebe just didn't believe this was intentional.

Ebe couldn't forget no matter how much they wanted to. They had been best friends living together in punk houses for decades, since before either of them was old enough to sign a lease. They met in line for a punk show in another city, when they were just babies. Marley and Ebe tried dating but decided they made better friends. Ebe wanted a Daddy, or a Mommy, and Marley wanted to get the shit kicked out of hir by a hot Sir. Fundamentally incompatible in leather, but best friends for life.

Ebe and Marley had founded the free radical paper together, Ebe's final year in college. They had financed the whole thing with the last of Ebe's student loans but had made Marley an equal partner because the idea had been joint. They worked together of the paper until the day that Marley went missing. They didn't make much in money, but earned a lot in social capital and after a couple of years were making enough to bring on Cratchet as an assistant. At first Cratchet was an unpaid intern, but they hung around long enough Marley and Ebe offered them an actual job. Cratchet did everything from correspond to writers and listen to Ebe go off on their political rants, to—if Ebe was honest—drafting most of the popular and accessible content the paper published.

Marley's death was fucked up and stupid, and mysterious and just like hir. Ze'd been doing so well getting clean, working hir ass off on the paper with Ebe, and then all of a sudden ze disappeared. Ebe knew something was wrong but no one believed them. Everyone else thought that Marley was out on some binge, but Ebe knew that Marley would never ever do that to them. Ebe had to wait the 72 hours before the police would let them file a report. Ebe didn't sleep the whole time, they just kept working on the paper, thinking that if they got the new issue out, Marley would be there. But Marley never came home, and Ebe had to finish that issue of the paper without hir. Death only made Ebe more committed to the cause, even more convinced that the world needed saving. And that holidays were irrelevant and even dangerous, because they keep everyone from focusing on fighting the capitalist hegemonic patriarchy. Friends stopped calling. Ebe knew that others found them impossible to be around, but that was just because everyone else was weak, less committed. Ebe decided that being around them must kick stuff up for people, like an embodiment of calling people out on their shit, maybe that's why no one was inviting them out to stuff anymore, they decided.

Ebe had come to New York for college, and Marley came too, even though ze never managed to finish hir GED like ze promised hirself ze would. When they started the paper it had been in Ebe's dorm room. They stole paper from the campus computer lab and copies from the copy center downtown in the business district. Marley was secretly living in Ebe's dorm room. Their roommate was a tool, and always at her boyfriend's dorm, so she didn't even notice the extra stowaway roommate. On the rare nights the roommate was back in the room—usually only if she and her boyfriend were fighting—Marley would take a small pack and go down to the basement of the dorm building. There were coin-operated washers and dryers and ze could slip behind them. There was lots of lint, some change if ze was lucky, and only once a rat. In the morning when their roommate left for her first class, Ebe would go downstairs and wake Marley.

The only thing that mattered was the revolution. Ebe was uncompromising in their politics. There was no grey area for them, just a solid commitment to social change. Ebe was adamant about an intersectional politic. It was awesome and exhausting to be so committed to making a better world, and kinda lonely since anyone who didn't walk the walk didn't ever make it into their inner circle. There was no compromising, no fun, no vacation. Ebe spent a lot of time being shady about those activists who had other jobs outside of the work, who were clearly committed to their bougie lifestyles like vacations, buying groceries instead of dumpstering, and seeing movies in the theaters. This made dating hard. Sometimes Ebe would make political exceptions for romance— well, not really romance, but play.

Ebe wasn't much for the mushy romantic types of things, but sometimes the itch got so strong they would suck it up and pay to get into one of the monthly queer dungeon play parties. They would play for a few hours, maybe get a phone number, sometimes friend them on the kinky internet social media site. Usually they'd just obsessively read the profiles without friending; looking at photos (hot), checking out the kinks they had listed (sometimes even hotter), but rarely pursuing anything. Ebe was too busy to let themself get distracted by that kind of thing; it wasn't worth it. Except when it was, but then they had to work even harder to make up for those periods of indiscretion. Marley always joked that Ebe was so puritanical with their work ethic—Ebe hated it when Marley joked with them that way. What was the point of being a sexual outlaw if the only way to get your rocks off or to find the kind of dynamic you wanted meant compromising your morals and commitment to the cause? Sometimes Ebe was fond of saying they were "in service to the Revolution" but the revolution was a shitty Master, and besides, they wanted a Daddy, not a Master, anyway.

After graduating from college, Ebe had found this old brownstone that was completely falling apart, it had roaches and rats and the only good thing about that was that the management company didn't give a shit about who lived there and even relaxed the 40x the monthly rent income requirement. Investors had bought up the block banking on gentrification, but then the economy tanked and they were left with properties that were losing money.

Of course Ebe and Marley thought of the repercussions of gentrification, but they rented the house and turned the place into the communal live/work space they had been dreaming of since running away to New York.

The house was amazing, and when they moved there the Free Paper flourished. They were writing zines and self-publishing anthologies of other radical queer thinkers. Everything was done in the basement. Ebe and Marley never got sick of working together; the tougher the project the more committed to it they became.

Everyone assumed they were a couple. Ebe and Marley considered each other platonic life partners. They were building a movement together—the business of the free paper, but more than that. The communal house was more than just a place to crash and work on the paper, it was its own ecosystem.

They painted the living room bright red and tacked show posters to the walls. Marley briefly dated a girl who worked at the hardware shop and while they were hooking up she would "accidentally" mix the wrong color of paint for customers and have to "throw out" the crayon-colored cans and remix the tan beige and soft grays. At the end of her shift Marley would pick her up and together they would carry the cans of Clementine Orange and Robin Egg Blue back to the old brownstone.

Marley and Ebe immediately let Cratchet and Tiny move in. They met when Ebe was working on a story about animal rights activists for the paper and interviewed Cratchet, who had just moved to New York from the Pacific Northwest. Out west, they had been really involved in some animal liberation group and decided it was time for a location change—after things started to heat up after a raid of an animal testing facility in southern Oregon where a bunch of beagles were being used for cosmetic testing. It was awful, the way Cratchet described it. They had to take a plea bargain for their role in the whole mess but lucked out not having parole and came to New York with Tiny. Tiny was the smallest dog that either Ebe or Marley had ever seen. At first they thought he was a rat—not a gross subway one, but the cute friendly ones that are so popular with travelers and crusty punks. Cratchet was from the west coast so it made sense that they would have a rat, only Tiny wasn't a rat; he was a chihuahua that Cratchet ended up with after he was liberated from a puppy mill. Cratchet's whole world revolved around Tiny and they were really clear about that when they interviewed for the room.

"Pretty much all I do is spend time with Tiny. You don't have to worry about me having overnight guests or anything. Really, my whole world revolves around this little man," Cratchet explained, smiling down at Tiny who was nestled into a baby sling across their chest.

A big part of why Cratchet had decided to come to New York was that getting caught liberating those beagles had really spooked them. Cratchet hadn't even been the one actually doing the liberating, but had been involved with the planning—that's how they slipped through without jail or parole. Cratchet told Ebe how they had been talking to an attorney and realized how deep in they were. There was no one who would take care of Tiny, and that's what made Cratchet panic and take the plea bargain. They refused to say if they had to testify against anyone. Marley always said that was probably the real reason why Cratchet left the west coast. They would have done anything to protect Tiny, maybe even rat folks out.

With Marley gone, Ebe was so alone. Cratchet was just downstairs but Ebe couldn't let themself get close to them. Ebe didn't want to intrude on the little world that Cratchet and Tiny had together. Despite how hard it was to meet anyone in this city, especially anyone with the right kinks and the right politics, Ebe was trying. Just last week this super hot Leather Daddy they knew from some sexual freedom coalitions, named Freddie, had taken them on another date with hys girl, Olivia. The three of them had been involved in a flirtation for months whenever they saw each other, and when Freddie approached Ebe about a date, they said "yes" before giving themself time to panic and change their mind.

They went to one of those pottery painting places that have jumped from strip malls into Brooklyn neighborhoods. They arrived at the shop at dinner time when the families with small children would be cleared out. They met out front on the frozen sidewalk. Ebe had been nervous and kept kicking their boot against a dented mailbox as they waited. Ebe thought about turning and ducking back into the subway. Marley was dead and the thought of doing something fun felt impossible and disrespectful. Ebe had known Freddie for a long time. Their courtship was a frustrating game of cat and mouse. Freddie wanted them. Ebe wanted Freddie too, and the leather family that came with hym, but Ebe wouldn't let themself go there. Dungeon play was one thing, and they and Freddie had been playing that game for a long time—blood, sex, tears...all that was easy when it came in the dark, with silicone and rawhide— but that wasn't what Ebe wanted, and it wasn't what Freddie wanted either.

Problem was, Ebe couldn't let themself go lifestyle. Wouldn't let themself have feelings, or surrender, or commitment. HUMBUG, they yelled in their head. SAFEWORD. They just couldn't. They couldn't let themself have deep feelings or be little. It was just too much. And yet they wanted it more than anything, and so they pushed through the panic and arrived at the pottery shop right on time.

Freddie and hys girl Olivia had also just arrived. Ebe could see them through the big shop window taking off their coats and hanging them on little hooks next to a big painting table. The shop window glowed warm and golden against the grey cold of the street. They paused for a moment and watched as Freddie squeezed hys girl's hand and ruffled her hair. This courtship was a package, a tangle of identities, and for the first time Ebe realized they might not be the only one who was afraid. Even Olivia, who by all accounts had the most to lose here: if this worked, if the fantasy they sometimes whispered about were to come true, she would have to share her Daddy. Ebe had asked Olivia about this once in the corner of a dungeon after the three of them had played:

"But why would you share something so precious?" Ebe had asked Olivia

"You mean besides the fact we're getting something so cute?"

Ebe blushed. They didn't want to, but couldn't help themself. It was always this way around these two. Somehow they broke down all of Ebe's walls with a laugh and a lollipop.

"Seriously," Ebe pressed, "aren't you worried that if Freddie and I...that your family would be ruined?"

Olivia, who usually wasn't much for seriousness, and instead was always babbling about the latest video game or comic book, took Ebe's hand and replied, "if I thought you wanted to hurt my Daddy I would break your face, but I see the way you look at hym and I know the way hy looks at you. Besides, I've always wanted a sister, and you and I have so much fun together! If you take Daddy's collar it could always be like this! I know I'm not losing my Daddy because of you, I don't think Daddy and I have ever been closer. If you move in, if you become part of our family, I'm gaining the sister I've always wanted. This is about getting more family, not less!"

That girl... Ebe still couldn't believe how lucky they were to have met Olivia and Freddie. They hated themself for not being able to fully trust them, or be half as kind as they were to them.

Ebe made themself get up extra early that morning so they would finish all their editing for the Free Paper before the date. They almost canceled anyway, but by then all the work was done so cancelling felt more wasteful, and they had already told Cratchet they were going out. The reindeer bells on the door jingled as Ebe opened the door of the pottery shop. The floor was the color of honey and Ebe's old boots left wet prints as they walked in. The shop smelled like paint and bubble gum and was swallowed by the sound of an internet radio station playing Christmas carols sung by pop stars. Why must everything be Christmas?! What a waste! Ebe hated Christmas, but didn't want to let that ruin the date. Ebe smiled as they walked towards Freddie and Olivia. Ebe was happy to see them, they wanted to be there, wanted to be with them, not just for this evening

"HUMBUG," Ebe yelled inside their head, eyes closed. No, they wouldn't let fears of tomorrow or the kind of commitment Ebe knew they couldn't promise ruin tonight's fun.

Freddie hugged them tight after they tossed their cargo jacket onto a bench. Ebe had worn a plain black dress and black leggings. They had almost worn a light pink dress they found months ago at a thrift store but had never worn. At the last minute they decided it felt too soft and changed into the worn black dress that felt like armor. They had tugged their hair into pigtails though. Olivia looked so happy to see them! She was wearing a red tshirt printed with characters from one of her favorite comic books in Santa hats, bright green tights, pink sneakers with rainbow shoe laces and a faded denim skirt. Ebe smiled and let Olivia take their hand and drag them across the shop to the shelves of chalky white ceramic figures in the shapes of dogs and elephants, piggy banks shaped like unicorns, and more practical things like coffee cups and plates. "Look Ebe, look!" Olivia squealed.

Ebe looked around the shop, feeling themself blush with embarrassment. Ebe was a bit shy and got anxious being around littles like Olivia who were so...unapologetic, so...authentic. God, Ebe hated that word. They hated most of all that they always felt like they were trying to be something, and falling short. The shop was empty. The only other customers were a young straight couple who sat at a small corner table and were each painting coffee cups. Every time they leaned forward to get more paint they kissed. They were definitely not paying attention.

Ebe let themself get swept away into the fun of looking at every funny shaped cup and animal figure with Olivia. They were vaguely aware of Freddie standing behind them watching, smiling. After they had looked at every shelf, Freddie walked up behind and put hys arms around both of their shoulders, before bending over to gently kiss the tops of their heads.

"You each may pick anything you want to paint from the middle shelf, " Freddie said, still standing between them and taking one of their hands in each of hys. The middle shelf had the medium sized pieces, and was the best one, thought Ebe. The middle shelf had all the characters and figures.

"Thank you Daddy!" squealed Olivia, pulling her hand loose from Freddie and going up close to the shelves again to pick the piece she wanted to paint.

Ebe picked a coffee cup. They were going to paint it for Freddie. Ebe knew they wanted hym as their Daddy, they wanted to be hys, but goddamn HUMBUG. Going there, surrendering completely, was just so impossibly hard. Olivia picked out a ceramic plate shaped like Santa's face.

"Daddy! I'm going to paint this so we can have a special plate to use when we leave cookies out for Santa!"

"That sounds like a great idea," Freddie replied. "Are you going to give him a green beard?"

"No, Daddy! Don't be silly. The green is for the holly leaves on his coat!" Olivia replied.

"I'm pretty sure being silly is my job..." Freddie replied, leaning over to tickle hys girl.

"Are you making a cup for Santa's milk?" Olivia asked Ebe who had just grabbed a bottle of purple paint from the shelf above the table. There was a speaker near them and a pop star Ebe didn't quite recognize was singing "Have Yourself a Merry Little Christmas."

Have yourself a merry little Christmas
Have yourself a merry little Christmas
Let your heart...
Merry little Christmas

HUMBUG

"I'm pretty sure that Santa wants something stronger than milk."

Olivia frowned and then bit her lip. Christmas mattered more than almost anything to Olivia, but it was no secret to her that Ebe struggled with it. No, struggle was too kind a word to describe the kind of hate that Ebe seemed to have, not just for the holiday but for everything it seemed to represent. In so many ways, this was Olivia's biggest concern about the possible relationship that was forming between the three of them. Just tonight before Ebe came, Olivia and Freddie had talked about the possible compatibility problems.

"Daddy they hate Christmas, and everything about the season!"

"They say they do," Freddie answered.

"And they act so mean and then safeword out!"

"HUMBUG. HUMBUG. HUMBUG!" Olivia whined in a mocking tone.

Freddie chose to ignore Olivia's rudeness and responded:

"Have you ever noticed, they act the same way about Christmas as they do when they get overwhelmed by how kind we are, or when conversations turn serious about us all being together? I know it's hard when they try to pick a fight about Christmas with you, but you care about them too, right?"

"I do, I really want them to be able to find a way to work through this and become ours. I remembered when all of this was so scary for me too, where I couldn't let you take care of me. Where everything you did that was nice was just too much, and so I would push you away." Olivia scuffed her boots along the sidewalk and fingered the loose edge of a sticker on her cell phone.

Freddie smiled. "I'm so proud of you," hy said as hy put hys hand under Olivia's chin, raising it to make her meet hys eyes. "I mean it, I'm so proud of how much you have grown, and how hard you are working to be a good sister to Ebe. If they're ready to make this commitment, it will be because you are living by example and being so kind to them."

"Santa is just embodiment of the patriarchy anyway. He's not real. He's a fantasy that people use to bribe children into compliance, and a glorification of consumerist gluttony," Ebe huffed.

Olivia bit her lip. She wanted to defend Santa, and the season, and more than that her little family, and how much this holiday mattered to them, how much she hoped someday it could matter to Ebe.

Ebe felt like such an asshole. Immediately they wanted to apologize to Olivia, who had been nothing but kind to them always, who wanted to build a family with them! HUMBUG

Freddie squeezed Olivia's knee under the table and changed the subject to dinner. Both Olivia and Ebe's tummies were rumbling.

They finished painting their pots. Freddie had decided on a "welcome home" plaque. Hy and Olivia shared a beautiful home together, one that they hoped to one day share with Ebe—there was space for them if only they could surrender to their own desires, to the idea that anyone could love them. If only they could believe that both Freddie and Olivia loved them very much and wanted to welcome them into the family.

The three ate at a diner down the street, squeezing into a little back booth, Freddie sitting between the littles. Both had ordered chicken strips and fries. Freddie laughed as they squealed and protested when hy insisted they also share a salad.

"Two of you, and not a vegetable between you! What's a Daddy to do?"

Freddie caught hys comment, calling hymself daddy to Ebe. Hy blushed at how forward hy was, though it wasn't as if the three hadn't had the conversation many times. Ebe's uncertainty was about owning and living their desires. Hy was uncertain whether they could let themself have something that they wanted so deeply. Whenever Ebe let themself get close to it, they froze, safeworded out not from anything Freddie was doing or saying, but from their own mind. Safeworded out of their own future.

Freddie's blush turned to a big grin when hy realized that Ebe hadn't corrected hym, or changed the subject.

"Vegetables might fuel the revolution, but not me!" Ebe replied, taking a dramatic dinosaur-style bite of their French fry, complete with teeth mashing and a growl!

Olivia laughed so hard that soda came out her nose.

The diner was playing classic Christmas carols. Freddie felt hys chest open and hys smile grow. This was the family hy wanted and in this moment the spirit of the season wrapped around the little family, enveloping them in playful love. Olivia and Ebe snuggled up to hym, one under each arm.

After dinner, as the trio left the diner, Olivia turned to Freddie and asked, "Daddy can Ebe come over and watch Christmas movies?"

"I'm not sure if that's something Ebe wants to do, but if they do, yes of course." Freddie replied.

"I need to get back to the collective, the new issue of the paper comes out tomorrow and I have a lot to do." Ebe had turned icy again; they had already proudly told Freddie over dinner how everything was done.

Olivia looked at Freddie, her smile falling. Christmas was a symbol of everything Ebe was convinced they should fight against. It represented the patriarchy. It was the embodiment of capitalism.

When Ebe got to the collective, there was band practice happening in the basement, so Cratchet was in the kitchen sitting at the table with their laptop while another roommate, Charles, stirred a pot of lentils on the stove. Cratchet was wearing mismatched wool socks that their ex-girlfriend knit for everyone in the house last winter when the boiler was broken, a pair of flannel pajama pants and an old black hoodie with big back patch of a dog paw and human fist raised together. The heat in the house was on the fritz again. The landlord claimed he would send someone by, but someone hadn't shown up yet and every morning this week they had been able to see their breath. Tiny was laying against Cratchet's chest, asleep in his wrap.

"Whatcha working on?" Ebe asked, backwards-straddling a kitchen chair. "The online fundraiser for Tiny!" Cratchet said excitedly. "We had another consultation with the vet tonight and they think he's a good candidate for surgery!"

"Oh, I thought you said you were going to work on that article about gaslighting in activist spaces," Ebe replied while ripping out the rubber bands that held their hair in pigtails and retying it in a messy bun.

"Yeah I know, I emailed you the draft earlier when you were out," Cratchet coldly replied, the irony of the conversation far from lost on them.

"And the one about microaggressions?" Ebe snapped

"I'll get there," Cratchet quietly replied. "I really want to get this fund-raiser up. It's almost Christmas and I know that everyone is broke, but the vet says the longer we wait the less likely it is that he will regain feeling. It will cost about $400 to get him a wheelchair-cart and another $2,000 for the surgery. Figure if the surgery and physical therapy works eventually we can donate the cart to another dog. Right, Tiny?" Cratchet asked scritching Tiny's mouse-sized black ears.

Ebe rolled their eyes. "I don't know why everyone spends so much money on Christmas, or on dogs." They were feeling angry and lashing out, they knew that. They had promised they wouldn't do that anymore, yet... "No offense, but doesn't it seem selfish to spend that kind of money on one dog, when a rescue or sanctuary could support so many dogs with that kind of money? Or better yet, give the money to people? I was just reading a blog about this European collective that is doing really good work with refugees. I could send you the link." Ebe finished.

They knew they were making everything worse even when they tried to help.

Cratchet stroked Tiny's body, and didn't reply. They'd had this fight with Ebe before, and knew there was no compromise or reasoning with them when they got like this.

"How was your date?" Cratchet asked, changing the subject.

Ebe blushed. "Fine, good, fun, weird. I don't know. I like both Freddie and Olivia so much, but they are like a fucking perverse Hallmark commercial. Like really, I don't understand the point of half of what they do this time of year. I remember watching them get a tree and decorate their house and shit last year but I didn't realize how serious they were about this stuff!" Ebe confessed. "I like them, but this Christmas nonsense is too much." Ebe felt their mood souring again.

"Did you fuck?" Cratchet asked. "Olivia isn't my type, but that Freddie is HOT. Hy could beat and fuck my ass any day."

"Nope."

"Why the hell not?!"

"It isn't about that between us, that isn't what I'm looking for with them, or even what they want from me."

"But hy is so hot!"

"Sure, but hy is also smart and committed and a brutal caretaker and that, that Big/little connection is what I want from them, what we all want. We've fucked a couple of times, like at the dungeon and stuff, but we're negotiating a life, not a scene. I might be ruining all of this, or maybe it's just an awful distraction from the cause."

"HUMBUG."

Ebe left the kitchen and went downstairs. The band was fucking around and didn't seem to be taking practice very seriously.

"How much longer will you be down here?" Ebe asked Boz, who lived in the little bedroom in the attic and was lead singer of the band.

"I guess we can be done," Boz said, taking a swig from a beer bottle by his feet. The practice space was also the newspaper office, and Boz knew well enough that fighting with Ebe wasn't how he wanted to spend his Friday night.

Ebe stayed up all night working on a new issue of the paper—they'd drafted outlines for articles about queer assimilation, the dangers of marriage equality, Santa Claus mythology as a tool for indoctrinating children, and a spotlight on a new radical mental health collective that was opening. Between the hours of 3 and 5 AM they sent Cratchet approximately 15 emails and grew increasingly irritated that they weren't responding. By the time Cratchet got downstairs at 10 AM dressed in an old flannel shirt and work plants, Tiny cradled in their arms, Ebe was extremely cranky.

"Glad you are making it to work today," they snapped as Cratchet stomped down the stairs. Cratchet glanced at the time on their cell phone and rolled their eyes. There was no arguing with Ebe when they got like this. Any attempt at calling out their behavior would only earn you a lecture about your lack of commitment to the movement. All you could hope to do was stay out of their way. Cratchet set Tiny on the floor and watched him shakily pull himself around the basement dragging his back legs behind him, and opened their laptop to see how many stories Ebe had assigned overnight.

Over the next week Ebe threw themself into their work on the paper. They hadn't been able to make themself go back to pick up the pottery, canceling their date with Freddie and Olivia on December 24th to go back as a group to get the ceramics they painted now that they had been fired. Well, they didn't exactly cancel, they just didn't show.

Ebe let themself get pulled into work. They spent all of their time in the basement of the collective. Most of the other members noisily drifted out, heading for busses and planes "home" to small towns and suburbs across the country. Soon, only Ebe and Cratchet were left at the collective. Over Christmas. Ebe was committed to spending the days working and churning out a new issue of the paper. Ebe was supposed to be at the pottery paint shop with Freddie and Olivia in a few hours. They weren't going. HUMBUG. Ebe had been ignoring their phone all afternoon.

Cratchet had to keep working or fear getting the wrath of Ebe's relationship issues directed at them. Cratchet knew their work and home life was dysfunctional but it wasn't like they had anywhere else to spend Christmas and they refused to get chased out of their own home, the one they had built, on a holiday just because Ebe was a dick. Besides, it hadn't always been this bad. Cratchet attributed most of it to Marley's death and how much that had made Ebe shut down and pull away from everything except for the newspaper. Cratchet worried that Ebe was pushing Freddie and Olivia away too, that relationship had been so good for them, or at least it seemed that way from the outside, but now it seemed like Ebe was looking for reasons to push them away too. Christmas was such a fraught season for Ebe. They had always hated it, always been nasty cold this time of year, but it was worse now than any year before. It was like Ebe couldn't see the good in the world, the joy in life anymore. They could only see what was bad. All of their energy went into trying to create this utopian revolution. They were shutting out everything real in the world. No matter how hard Cratchet or anyone else worked, they were never good enough for Ebe, never radical enough, never committed enough. It wasn't inspiring, it was sad. Ebe was so committed to community, and yet had long ago forgotten that generosity was something to be valued.

Cratchet's whole life was Tiny—getting him to different appointments and play dates, cooking for him, consulting online message boards of other guardians of medically fragile dogs. Cratchet had a family. With Tiny they had a little home, not just in the collective but in their room, the little haven they had built for themself and Tiny. Cratchet also had a life outside the paper. To cover Tiny's medical bills, they had started dog walking a few months back and now had a really steady route going. Tiny got to go to work with them zipped into their hoodie. When they saw Cratchet going out to work, a thick ring of keys bouncing against their hip, Ebe always had something smart to say about the bougie yuppies who spent money to pay Cratchet to walk their dogs, but Cratchet ignored Ebe's comments about that just like they did Ebe's comments about most other things. Cratchet mostly just felt sorry for them. After all, what did Ebe have? They could have a home and the kind of dynamics they had always talked about wanting with Freddie and Olivia, but Cratchet was more and more doubtful that they could allow themself to ever have that. It would mean Ebe would have to let go, they would have to find joy and generosity of spirit. In short, they would have to stop putting the construction of a radical utopia ahead of everything, they would have to find magic in the world and allow themself to be embraced by it.

Ebe had ignored their phone all day, but as Cratchet stood and stretched, yawned and said, "I'm going to take Tiny out for a walk before it gets colder," Ebe scowled and picked up their phone. It was blowing up. Ebe ignored the voicemails like always and started scrolling the texts.

> **Freddie:** Fri 2:04pm
> **Hey darlin- we still on for 8?**

> **Freddie:** 4:19pm
> Hope your day is ok just wanting to make sure plans for tonight are still ok?

All afternoon as Cratchet worked they had heard Ebe's phone ringing, but knew better than to ask about the incoming text messages that they knew weren't being answered. Tiny lay spiraled in a blanket in a small dog bed balanced on the big drafting table, where Cratchet worked laying out the new issue of the newspaper. For the past two years Cratchet and Ebe had been working on saving money in order to upgrade to a computer program that wouldn't require them all to print everything out and then layout by hand. The new computer programs and the computers they would need to run them were so expensive. Cratchet didn't think they would ever be able to afford them, but Ebe'd had an idea. They had started selling ads in the paper, which was kinda fucked and capitalistic, but they were only selling the ads to local radical businesses like vegan bakeries and tattoo shops and feminist bookstores. Ebe had managed to save up $5,000. They were so close to being able to afford the new equipment they both could almost taste it. Every week when the ad money came in, Ebe would cash the checks at the bank and put the cash into a plastic lunchbox with 80s cartoons on the cover that they had found in the side of the road one trash day.

Ebe's phone had been on the counter by the stairs all afternoon and evening, and they hadn't done more than give the screen a quick glance. At the top of the stairs Cratchet turned around, seeing Ebe looking at their phone, and smiled.

"I'm taking tomorrow off."

"Why?" Ebe responded, looking up from their phone.

"It's kinda the norm for Christmas don't you think?"

"A poor excuse for abandoning the movement," Ebe snapped and looked back at their phone.

Missed call from Freddie 7:30pm

Olivia: 8:03pm

We really missed you tonight! My Santa plate turned out really good! I didn't let them show me your cup — wanted you to see it first. Daddy and I hope you are ok. Miss you.

Freddie: 8:10pm

It's Christmas Eve, I know Christmas is so hard for you but Olivia and I are really disappointed to not hear from you.

Freddie: 9:03pm

I would order you to respond to me, we've talked about how that is one of my expectations for anyone in service to me, but right now, I'm having a hard time knowing where we stand... Do you want me to order you to contact me? Is that what this is about? I don't play games. I'm not going to do that.

Olivia: 10:44pm

Daddy and I are about to bake gingerbread for Santa. I wish you were here. Remember you were going to the dungeon party with us and then spend the night and try to convince my Daddy to let us stay up to see if we could see Santa?

HUMBUG. Ebe silenced their phone. They had talked to Olivia about those plans but they hadn't finalized them. Ebe said they would think about it, they hadn't promised anything. Besides, they didn't get Freddie or Olivia any Christmas presents. HUMBUG.

Ebe shut down their computer and walked upstairs. The kitchen, usually a gathering place of all the punks, was empty with everyone else in the house away visiting bio family. HUMBUG. Ebe made themself a simple dinner, some bread someone had dumpstered from behind the bakery, pasta and some veggies that had gone a little soft from someone's CSA. They sliced the carrots and zucchini and threw them into the boiling pot. It wasn't until Ebe had strained the pasta and thrown the tomato sauce on top that they remembered the date two weeks ago, with Freddie and Olivia, the joking about vegetables and how Daddy—how Freddie would be so proud of them for eating some tonight. Ebe pulled the purple scarf tighter around their shoulders. They were wearing a thin orange sundress with anti-capitalism and anti-war patches sewn near the hem. It was cold being alone in the house.

Part 2:
Remembering

Ebe put the pot they had used to cook into the sink. They dropped it with more force than intended and heard the cracking of china as the pot fell. "Wasteful," they admonished themself, but left the broken plate. Ebe carried their dinner up the dark stairs towards their bedroom.

As they reached to open their door, Ebe's eyes were drawn to the faded poster that hung amongst other newspaper clippings, bumper stickers, and protest flyers. It was a poster from Marley's old band in SF, from before ze had moved to New York. On the poster the band was behind hir, and Marley was center stage with hir hot pink guitar, wearing short shorts, fishnets and a crop top that said "muffin top" with hir belly rolls spilling out from underneath. It was Ebe's favorite picture of Marley, even though ze still had hir green dreads that Ebe had finally convinced hir were appropriative and made hir shave off. Ebe hung the poster on their door when they moved out of the dorm and into the collective, and even after Marley died Ebe couldn't make themself take it down.

Tonight, though, they were spooking. As they stood at their door it looked like Marley's hands were moving. Ebe shook their head but sure enough Marley's chipped nails were strumming chords on hir guitar, and then they heard the iconic chords of the start of the band's signature song.

Ebe stepped away from their door, trying to remember when they had last slept or if they had taken anything today. This was not their idea of a good trip. But Ebe was sober.

They stared at Marley's paper face and watched as the faded paper shifted and the paper Marley turned to face them. And then, hir mouth opened.

"Hey Ebe..." Hir voice was raspy, like ze just smoked a whole pack, just the way that Ebe always remembered it.

Ebe grabbed the knob of their door, twisted and pulled hard. The old door sticky with decades of paint finally opened and Ebe had to slam it behind them to get it to close. Their bedroom was how it always was, sparse and mostly neat. Ebe had a little bed in one corner and a desk under the window piled with old copies of the paper. The walls were papered with flyers from shows and protests alongside covers of some of their favorite issues of the paper. Spooked by the vision of Marley, Ebe set their dinner down on the desk and carefully walked to the closet. Nothing, other than piles of old dresses on the floor. Ebe made a mental note that they should put up a post on the local queer trading site to get some hangers.

Relieved there was no sign of their dead friend, Ebe returned to their dinner. They ate it in bed, the most comfortable spot to sit, after having set the needle onto their favorite record, a recording of a 90s riotgrrrl band who just released their greatest hits on vinyl. The paper had published a review so Ebe had gotten the records for free. One of the perks of the work.

You know that feeling like someone is watching you? Ebe had that feeling. The hairs on their arm stood up as they shoved a forkful of pasta into their mouth. They hadn't heard the door open, so Ebe knew they were alone. Besides, Cratchet was the only other collective member still in town and they were out with Tiny, looking in on some dogs they were walking over the holiday. Ebe concentrated on chewing their food. They were tired, they were stressed about having ignored the texts from Freddie and Olivia all day and what this would mean for the future of their relationship. They wanted to be in service to Freddie, they wanted to be leather siblings with Olivia, but HUMBUG that was such a sellout thing to want. That was the hardest thing for Ebe. At least it was a poly 24/7 leather dynamic that they wanted. If it had been something less radical that would have made the whole thing even worse, but still even this level of domesticity, settling down, commitment... Ebe knew they were overthinking things, spinning out. They were good at that, always had been. They twitched, feeling the anxiety course through them. Finally, even though they knew it was stupid, and that they were alone in the room, Ebe turned around.

Marley was standing behind them, watching. Ebe dropped the bowl and closed their eyes.

"This can't be happening. You're dead!" Ebe whispered, opening their eyes. Marley was still standing in their room. Ze looked foggy like a poorly developed Polaroid. Marley wore a bondage chest harness, and ankle and wrist cuffs—high quality, nice bondage gear like the kind they used to go and look at in the leather shops down on Christopher Street when they first moved to NYC, back when the village was still gay and gritty. Now it seemed like it was all high-rise condos and straight hipsters.

"I'm having a breakdown," Ebe said, almost calmly. "That's what it must be. That's all that makes sense. I've been putting too much pressure on myself to make a decision about Freddie and Olivia. I've cracked."

"You are as sane as you ever were," Marley responded.

"I can't be or you wouldn't be here in my bedroom. Or rather, you aren't here of course, but I wouldn't be thinking you were here, and I certainly wouldn't be talking with some imagined ghost of my best friend."

"I'm here, I'm as real as I've ever been, and I want to help you."

"HUMBUG!"

"Darlin', you can't safeword out of this."

"Why the fuck not!? That's the whole point of a safeword!"

"Sweetie, you and I have never played very safe. Remember that time at the dungeon in San Francisco when—"

"Yes, of course I remember that," Ebe responded, cutting Marley off. "But you were actually alive then, doing stupid hot reckless shit. Are you trying to tell me you aren't dead?"

"No, I'm dead but that doesn't mean I'm not here. It's important we talk, and we don't have much time."

"What do you mean we don't have much time, if you are really here talking with me, which I'm still pretty sure is me having some kind of visual and auditory hallucination, then we have all the time in the world. You're dead! What else could you possibly have to do!? Are you organizing protests on the other side? Are you feeding the homeless? Are there homeless on the other side!?" Ebe was getting frantic again.

"Ebe, listen to me," Marley broke in. "There is more to life than the revolution, than the fight. You can work to make the world a better place without destroying your life in the process. You don't have to isolate yourself like this. You don't have to cut people off who want to love you, to prove how committed you are to fighting the patriarchy or systematic oppression."

"You're one to talk! We built this paper together. Everything we did was for the good of the movement!" Ebe responded.

"I was wrong—not about the work itself," Marley added quickly when it looked like Ebe might lunge or argue or puke, the veins in their neck pulsing. "But I was wrong to give it so much power and control in my life. I was wrong to make it the most important thing I did—to focus on the work but never on my relationships with others. It's too late for me, but it doesn't have to be for you."

"My life is pretty awesome right now," Ebe protested.

"Is it?"

"The paper is doing better than ever. We have a new web presence and are getting hits from all over the world. We are interviewing major activists and doing on-the-ground work supporting protests against police brutality, and transphobic policies on college campuses, and the lack of shelter beds."

"That's all really important work, but it isn't the only thing that matters."

Ebe rolled their eyes and Marley continued.

"Tonight, you will have three more visitors. I wish I could say it would be easy; consider this your trigger warning. These visitors are going to upset you. I hope they scare you. I don't want you to end up like me, filled with so much regret for everything I never did. I gave to everyone but those closest to me. I was so committed to all of these causes fighting the patriarchy that I pushed everyone away and now here I am...alone. " Marley's voice cracked and hir blurrier appearance got even hazier.

"Can't you stay?" Ebe asked quietly, pleading.

"I wish I could, but you have a long night ahead of you... You can't run away. The first visitor will arrive at one."

If Marley had looked like a poorly developed Polaroid when ze arrived, as ze left everything became even more transparent until ze was gone and Ebe was again left alone in their room. They didn't pick up the cracked bowl on their floor or the spilled dinner. "Let the roaches have it," Ebe thought to themself. Ebe kept thinking about Marley's message, how ze hadn't wanted to talk about how ze died. Ebe couldn't decide if they thought the ghost of Marley had been real or not. Their uncertainty about that was scary. Ebe was worried that they were losing their grip. "Ghosts aren't real. Ghosts aren't real. Ghosts aren't real," they whispered to themself over and over again as they pulled on their pajamas—an old flannel pair of pants that had been patched so many times it was hard to discern what was the original pattern was, and a hoodie they were given when they started college. They didn't wear it anywhere but to bed in the big drafty house, because Ebe didn't like to advertise that they'd been to an Ivy League. They got a good education, and gained so many tools for understanding capitalism and systemic oppression, but still, they were embarrassed about the access they had to get there, even though it was all they had ever wanted growing up and Ebe had busted their ass to get good enough grades to make it in.

Ebe crawled into bed and pulled the worn blanket over their head. They hadn't hidden in bed like this since they were a little kid. If they couldn't see anyone, then no one else could see them. Mercifully, they fell into a fitful sleep almost right away. The last issue of the paper had been keeping them so busy they had barely slept at all in days, and even though their mind was on overdrive their body took over and knocked Ebe out.

Ebe awoke once, still freaked out about having seen Marley. After all, it's not every day your dead best friend shows up in your bedroom to have a little chat. Ebe was convinced it was stress that was finally getting to them—stress from losing Marley and not being able to make a decision about Freddie and Olivia and if they could move forward with taking that relationship to the next level, whatever non-assimilationist patriarchal level that could look like, or if they even fucking wanted to. Freddie and Olivia's home and family were so lovely but they were also a distraction. They kept Ebe's focus away from the revolution, the paper, the real work that they needed to be solidly committed to. If they didn't do this work, who would? Everyone else could goof off, fall in love, play, fuck, travel. They didn't understand how important all this work was, how essential it was, that Ebe needed to fight the fight, all the fights. Human liberation, animal liberation, systemic hegemonic patriarchy, homophobia, transphobia, racism, classism, ableism, it was all so related and if Ebe wasn't fighting all of those all the time, then they were just wasting time and resources that should go to the fight. To Ebe it was so clear, and also an endless loop: what they shouldn't be doing, what they should be doing all the time, in every situation, to live the most of their anti-oppression politic, to "walk the walk," as one of their professors had said once.

Some people could take or leave their activism, but not Ebe. It was all or nothing for them, and if given that choice, they were going to be in it all the way.

Ebe pulled the blankets over their head. They thought of what Marley—if it really was Marley and not their imagination—had told them.

"There will be three visions. You can't avoid them. They are coming for you, Ebe. Listen to them, please do it for me. If you don't listen to their messages and change your life, you are heading for my fate. Dead or alive, you will be alone. Your activism cannot save you. The revolution doesn't love you."

HUMBUG HUMBUG HUMBUG

Ebe wanted the memory of Marley to go away. This wasn't how they wanted to remember their best friend, trapped somewhere between the here and the there, trapped by the ideologies that ze was so committed to in life but now haunted and imprisoned by in hir death. The movement was all that had mattered. If Ebe didn't change the world, if they didn't keep the focus on the fight, then what was the point of anything? *Disturb the comfortable. Comfort is a sign of selling out,* was the last thing Ebe remembered thinking before they fell asleep.

Ebe awoke at 1:00, hearing the beeping of their computer alerting them to new emails arriving in their inbox. Before Ebe could think about climbing out of bed to see which listserve was active tonight, there, standing at the foot of their bed was a figure. Ebe tried to scream, but no sound came. Even if it had, Ebe realized no one would hear them. There was no one in the house except for Cratchet and their room was three floors down.

The figure was dressed all in white—white skinny jeans and a tshirt clung to the androgynous frame. The figure wore a thick studded belt, and their arms were alive with bright tattoos of holly branches. They had a bright red beard covered in green glitter. The room was dark, but the figure seemed to glow as though Ebe's room had been turned into a club and they were illuminated by black light. The white clothes glowed and Ebe realized they were staring. The figure looked like a queer Jesus, or perhaps like one of the radical faeries that Ebe and Marley had written an article about a few years back when they were working their way through covering all the different queerlands across the United States, also known as an awesome excuse for a road trip/tour for Marley's band.

"This can't be happening," Ebe whispered, trying to calm themself, closing their eyes, and taking deep breaths. The therapist—whom they'd only seen twice—had tried to teach them how to do it in order to attempt to control their panic attacks, but the therapist hadn't gotten their pronouns and Ebe felt trapped like a bird with clipped wings in that dude's office, so they never went back.

"I'm still here," the figure responded.

Ebe peeked out from between their fingers, and saw the figure glowing at the edge of their bed.

"Who are you?" they asked.

"I am Christmas Past. You were told I was coming. You should have been expecting me."

Ebe didn't respond.

"We have much to see and not much time. Come!" the spirit ordered. As much as Ebe did not want to get out of their bed, as if ordered by a super powerful leatherdaddy, Ebe felt themself surrender, felt themself drift out of the bed and towards the spirit. They blinked and suddenly found themself outside, standing next to a snow bank, the spirit next to them.

Ebe immediately recognized the rundown building they stood in front of and didn't want to go in. They fell to their knees like they hadn't since the last time Marley had dragged them to the play party in that basement in Brooklyn. The familiar sensation of knees cracking against concrete. Ebe was a little but fought submission and didn't like being on their knees. But here, on the snowy sidewalk, they begged the spirit.

"Please, please don't let me remember. Please don't make me revisit this. I don't want to go back. I never want to go back here. I've worked so hard to make sure that I never had to."

The ghost did not speak, but instead reached out their small tattooed hand, lifting Ebe to their feet and through the door. For such a small being, the spirit was shockingly strong. Ebe didn't want to follow this ghost and yet they did. Ebe knew there was no resisting, there was no turning back.

The room was crowded and lively. Christmas carols played from a cassette player in the corner and everywhere was the sound of of laughter. Children tumbled out from under a wiry fake Christmas tree. The tree was rusted and the plastic needles had fallen off in clumps, but it was decorated with popcorn strings and a faded rainbow of ornaments made from popsicle sticks, paper and paste. Under the tree was piled high with little boxes. Each had a pink or blue construction paper Christmas tree taped to the top like a bow. The paper trees had been hung at the shopping center downtown where shoppers could pull one down and purchase a gift for a poor little boy or girl who was a ward of the state. Ebe had seen the tree walking back to the children's center from school, and saw a child in good sneakers standing next to the tree with his mom. Ebe knew those tags meant they and their friends would get Christmas presents. Ebe had crept closer, wanting to know whose tag the family would take, who was guaranteed a gift. "This is stupid. I don't want to buy a present for someone I don't know," the boy said. Ebe remembered how their face had flushed.

"But you have so many nice things. Think about other little boys and girls who don't have anything to open this Christmas. It's the spirit of the season to give," his mother replied. The boy rolled his eyes and pulled a little blue tree off the tree at random. He crumpled it in his hand as he and his mom headed towards the toy aisle. Ebe's face flushed with shame and anger.

"Do you know this place?" The spirit asked

"I don't want to," Ebe replied, their fists knotting at their side. Shivering, they tried to turn to go back out the door. Walking home through the snow and the years seemed a far better idea than staying here in this room a moment longer. As Ebe turned to leave, the spirit didn't move but Ebe's eyes were drawn down a little hallway just to the right of the door. The floor soft, and rotting below the cracked and duct-taped gold linoleum, bowed under their feet. Ebe didn't turn back to the party, to the children who squealed as they raced around the institutionalized living room. They didn't want to see the staff sitting in corners flipping through magazines and gossiping amongst each other.

At the end of the hallway was a small room lined with bunk beds. Ebe tried to turn around and flee, but the spirit was right behind them blocking the escape, and steered them into the bedroom. Sitting on the top bunk was a young Ebe wearing jeans and a faded tshirt from a city-sponsored summer program. A purple spiral notebook ragged with the edges of ripped out pages was spread across their lap. Looking closer, Ebe could see textbooks stacked at their side. The young Ebe was concentrating hard on an assignment, a chewed and sharpened nub of a yellow number two pencil in their teeth. The young Ebe didn't look up as another child, wearing a red and green paper chain around her neck, ran into the room, sliding in her stockinged feet.

"Come join the party. Miss Karen says it's almost time to open our presents!"

"No thanks, I have a lot of homework to do," the young Ebe replied, not even looking up from their notebook.

"But it's Christmas vacation!" the girl persisted.

"Maybe for you, but I'm studying. I'm going to go to college and I don't have time for presents."

"You are not! You're ten and you are in Mr. Brown's 4th grade class. You aren't in college."

"Stupid. Not yet I'm not, but I will be someday, so long as I study hard now!"

The argument could have continued back and forth, but the workers in the living room called out that it was time for presents. The little girl abandoned Ebe and raced back to get in line for her gift.

*

Ebe awoke tangled in their bedsheets. Although the room was cold, they were drenched in sweat. Ebe looked around but the room was just as they left it, tidy, dark, and quiet. They shivered and looked at the glowing lock-screen clock on their phone. If Marley were alive they would have texted hir, maybe. Ebe didn't want to be alone but they knew that they also would have been far too embarrassed to share this story with anyone. What would they have said? "I've been haunted and someone is showing me all the fucked up things that have happened on Christmas. " Really?

Ebe thought they sounded crazy. Or high. If they didn't know better they would think someone had laced their cigarettes, but they gave up smoking a few months back. Not because of the threat of lung cancer, but because continuing to smoke meant giving money to the tobacco industry that preyed upon kids, especially low income kids, and queer kids.

Ebe didn't know if sleep or consciousness was more frightening. They looked around, their breathing heavy and rapid, the beginnings of panic. HUMBUG HUMBUG HUMBUG. Ebe's mind was racing. They couldn't make things slow or quiet. They felt the room spin, and their chest ache. Ebe hated panic.

HUMBUG. There was the spirit again, coming towards their bed. Ebe couldn't read their facial expression. Maybe pity? Maybe... hopeless. Ebe didn't know what to think, if they could trust them, if they could believe any of this was even happening. Ebe watched as the spirit extended their pale holly-branch-tattooed arm towards them. The spirit's nails were painted alternating red and green glitter.

"Please no more, spirit. I'm so tired," Ebe whispered.

The spirit smirked. "The night has only just begun. You don't get to be tired yet."

Ebe was momentarily taken aback. From a lover, that kind of sentence would be so attractive—it was the kind of power play that turned them on, and got them in trouble. But in this case, coming from a total stranger who had so rudely appeared in their bedroom, Ebe wanted to curse this spirit out, and then Ebe wanted to tell the spirt that they were invalidating their embodied experience, that telling them how to feel was a microaggression. But, they kinda couldn't argue with a... deity? Angel? Demon? Ghost? Hallucination? Ebe realized they were really out of their league tonight—they didn't even know exactly what it was that was haunting them, and if it was real or not.

Ebe felt themself being pulled forward but their eyes were so heavy. Ebe felt them close... just for... a... minute and then suddenly everything was loud and as their eyes opened the room was so bright. They were no longer in their bedroom in the collective house. Ebe was disoriented and confused.

"Where am I?" they asked the spirit. "Where have you taken me now?!"

"You know where you are. We've come to visit a different past Christmas..." The spirit's voice trailed off. Ebe's eyes had started to adjust to the brightness of the room. It was a strange room. The walls were peeling, but covered with posters, HIV prevention messages, rules, rainbows. It was a community center, not just any community center, it was the LGBTQ youth community center that they had gone to as a young queer kid. Ebe's eyes darted from the make-shift kitchen in one corner, to the stuffed bookshelf next to the door. Just then, they saw the most beautiful grrrl walk in. She was tall, and thick. Ebe swallowed hard. They had forgotten how gorgeous this grrrl was—a serious punk princess.

"Bee..." Ebe whispered.

"You know her?" the spirit replied.

"Please spirit, please, please HUMBUG HUMGUG I can't take this. Don't make me watch this. I said I couldn't handle the other Christmas vision, but I *really* can't handle this one. I don't want to see what you are going to show me."

"And *that* is exactly why you need to," the spirit responded, right as a younger version of Ebe walked in the door behind Bee.

It was then that Ebe noticed the Christmas lights strung around the space, and the small tree on the pallet coffee table next to the frankenstein couch.

"No, please... not this Christmas..." Ebe whispered, but there was no safewording out.

Powerlessly Ebe watched as Bee curled up on the couch. She was wearing a red corset that accentuated the web of honeycomb tattooed in golden ink across her growing breasts and hips. Under the corset she wore a patchwork green corduroy skirt—kinda hippy except for the artful slit that revealed the swarm of wasps tattooed on her thigh. And, of course, her black boots with glitter gold toes.

Bee radiated the kind of serenity that Ebe lusted after—lusted in that way where it was almost impossible to determine where desire to *have* starts, and desire to *be*, ends. Bee said it was all the yoga she did, and the meditation retreats in the woods with goddess-loving lesbians who welcomed her into womanhood. Ebe could never quiet their mind enough to meditate, and was too dysphoric to sit in their body long enough to try yoga.

"Come to Mama," Bee purred to the young Ebe, who stood awkward at the doorway in work pants and an old tshirt. They clearly hadn't gotten the memo that this was a dress-up kinda day. Or, Ebe shuddered, they hadn't cared, even though it clearly mattered to Bee.

Young Ebe walked across the room towards Bee, who pulled from the folds of her skirt a sprig of mistletoe, a leather collar and heart shaped padlock. Young Ebe sat on the couch next to Bee, looking pale and nervous.

"Merry Christmas, little one," Bee whispered.

"Merry Christmas, Ma'am," Ebe responded, eyes darting between the collar and the mistletoe and Bee's clevage.

This was the moment—the moment young Ebe had dreamed of, belonging to someone, being their good girl, serving them...

"Oh Ma'am, not now. I mean, not now please? I mean, I want this, but I have so much to do right now. Food Not Bombs, the zine fest, Marley and I are going to start a radical political paper, and I'm organizing a radical queerleader contingency for the anti-corporate pride, and helping out at the anarchist cafe, and organizing with letters to prisoners... I want to be your girl more than anything, but I just need more time to get some of this work under control."

Bee held the collar out towards young Ebe, her eyes filling with tears.

"Ebe, you said this last year when I asked. I want to respect your request for more time, but I can't wait forever. I don't think you really want a Mommy or a Mistress. No, actually, I think you already have one and her name is the Revolution." Bee's glittery gold nails caught in the light of the Christmas tree as her hand, and the collar, fell back to her lap. Time froze.

Ebe recoiled from the scene like a horror movie, but there was no escaping it, or what was coming next. Young Ebe sat as far away from Bee as they could on the little couch. How had they gotten here? How had everything gotten so broken? Ebe wondered.

Ebe remembered meeting Bee at the anarchist bookstore and following her around like a lovesick puppy. Months later Bee confessed, while fucking them in the bathroom of a dive bar around the corner, that she had loved the way that Ebe followed her, and had only been pretending to ignore them. Normally Ebe wasn't much for those kinds of relationship games, but Bee was a punk rock princess, this was her aesthetic, and it was intoxicating. Ebe never could get enough, until the time came to commit. "Shit or get off the pot!" Ebe scolded themself.

Ebe remembered hearing someone, maybe Freddie say, "The leather community is so small sometimes." Ebe interrupted their own thoughts, they remembered hearing that Bee had moved out west. Portland? San Francisco? Ebe couldn't remember, all they knew for sure was that Bee was gone. Gone because all those years ago they hadn't been willing to make any political sacrifice, hadn't been able to set any boundaries with the Revolution. Being a part of every working group, every coalition, every committee, every protest, didn't leave much time for the kind of relationship they wanted. It didn't leave much time to have any relationships at all. And here Ebe was reliving that moment where they made that choice, the biggest regret they could never admit.

Part 3: Disassociation

Ebe woke to the buzz of their phone on the bedside table. It took them a moment to realize who and where they were. The nightmare of the group home and then the community center, and that spirit, so vivid. They reached over, feeling for their phone. The screen glowed bright and kinda blue. 2:09am. They slid the lock screen off and saw there were texts from Olivia: a picture. She was at The London, the dungeon downtown that Ebe and Marley used to try to go to when they first moved to New York. Freddie was on the programming board and so one of the big things hy organized every year—with Olivia's help, of course—was an annual Christmas party. A gathering for leather freaks and queers and anyone who needed community, connection, and maybe a good beating.

In the picture, Ebe could make out an artificial black glitter Christmas tree covered in rainbow ornaments. There was someone dressed up as Santa getting their boots blacked by an elf. Someone else in the background was strung up on a Saint Andrews cross bound in strings of lit Christmas lights.

It was a cute picture. Olivia had put a lot of work into the party and it was so like her to send the photo without any other message. Just a cute picture, no mention of the canceled date or Ebe's refusal to answer earlier messages. It was so cute Ebe could almost imagine Olivia giggling, running about, handing out candy canes to all the party guests.

"HUMBUG."

Enough Ebe thought. Enough. And slammed their phone back on the table. They rolled over and closed their eyes tight, hoping for sleep, true sleep. They tried not to think of Marley's prediction, that more visions were coming. Ebe wished they still had sleeping pills stashed in their bathroom. This would be a good moment to blackout, to not feel. They wanted to be alone, they wanted to drift into darkness and not be tortured by any more images.

It was light and laughter that next filled Ebe's room. They tried to feign sleep, pressing their eyes tighter together until all they could see was the red on the inside of their eyelids as the room grew brighter. Finally Ebe could resist no more and opened their eyes. In front of them was a vision unlike anything they had ever seen, aside from on the internet. The spirit was Ebe's height, but in the form of a porcelain doll. "Little Lolita." Ebe remembered seeing photos on the little blogs during the cherry blossom festivals, and complaints on message boards about how long it took to order those kinds of dresses from Japan.

The doll-like spirit was perched on the windowsill and light seemed to radiate from her smooth brown skin. She wore an ornate dress covered in lace and images of teddy bears having tea parties. Underneath the dress she wore a full pastel pink crinoline, white lace socks and black little ballet flats with ribbons that laced up her calves. In her hair, nestled into shiny mircobraids, was a huge pink and white seersucker striped bow.

The doll spirit was drinking from a fragile looking china teacup with a delicate rose pattern painted onto it.

"Oh good, you're awake," the spirit said in a little and playful voice.

"W-who are you?" Ebe whispered.

"I am the spirit of Christmas present. I am joy, and fun, and magic and whimsy. I know that you are familiar with littles..."

Ebe blushed.

"So you and I should get along just fine. But we haven't time to sit here and babble. There is so much to see, so much to do!"

The spirit set her teacup down on the windowsill, stood, holding her hand out to Ebe. Her short nails were painted a pearly pink and tiny rhinestones had been infused to the tips. Ebe took her cool, smooth hand, and they were off!

Their first stop was not far, just down the stairs and into the bedroom behind the kitchen. Cratchet's room. Ebe never spent much time in Cratchet's space. There was a small bed, a chair, a desk, and not much more. They noticed that under the window Cratchet had pinned up stockings. A little red one had "Tiny" stitched on all messy, since the only other thing they ever sewed was patches onto denim vests. Next to Tiny's red stocking was a green one with Cratchet's name written onto the white top in black sharpie.

To many, the room would have looked sad. It was just a boi and a dog curled up together under a blanket, Tiny's head pressed against Cratchet's chest as they stared at the little window, watching the blinking of the rainbow Christmas lights Cratchet had strung around the window frame. The radio was on, playing a Christmas carol.

Ebe hated Christmas carols and would never let Cratchet play them in the shared work space, or if Ebe momentarily relented they would mock the songs so completely that any joy in having them on was sucked out of the room. Ebe had always taken pleasure in calling out the fucked capitalistic heteronormative, patriarchal fantasy that those Christmas carols perpetuated, but watching Cratchet sitting quietly with little Tiny, Ebe felt something inside them quake. Living your values mattered. It mattered a lot. If you didn't uphold your beliefs, how could you expect anyone else to? How could you create systemic change? How could you inspire revolution? How could you change the world?

Ebe was lost in their self-indulgent political panic when they noticed Tiny try to move. He had been quietly playing with the edge of the blanket. Cratchet noticed and smiled, turning the worn fleece edge into a tug toy. Tiny shook the corner in his tiny jaws, growling like a mouse-sized lion. Cratchet laughed and smiled. Ebe also felt their face stretch into a smile, watching them play. While going for the tug, Tiny tripped on the fold of the sheet, his back legs giving out.

Ebe gasped watching the little dog, so full of life, stumble onto his face. Ebe looked to the spirit, but the spirit was watching Crachet and wouldn't meet their gaze. Ebe turned back, and saw that Cratchet was smiling down at Tiny. The dog lifted his little body up with his front legs and immediately dived for the corner of the blanket, radiating joy.

Ebe smiled. "Spirit, Tiny... Is he..." They couldn't quite bring themself to finish the sentence, but the spirit just stood waiting, pressing her lipstick'd creamy pastel pink lips together.

Ebe gathered their nerve. "Spirit, is Tiny going to die?"

"Everyone is dying, some just more quickly than others—but I don't think that's what you were asking." The spirit paused. "Without help, without access to better veterinary care and support, yes, Tiny will die."

"No! HUMBUG! No, spirit please, tell me that isn't true!" Ebe's eyes darted between the spirit's floral petticoats, and Tiny and Cratchet who, unaware of their presence, had continued their game of blanket tug. Tiny's needle teeth sunk into the green fleece as Cratchet laughed and gently tugged back on the blanket. The internet radio played carols from Cratchet's laptop. As the spirit steered Ebe out the door of Cratchet's room and out of the house into the cold night, they could hear Cratchet start to sing along.

"Have yourself a merry little Christmas..." was accompanied by small barks.

Ebe felt themself pulled along. It was windy and dark. It was as though they were flying through the night. The traffic of cars and busses whizzed past and the spirit dragged them on. As they drifted out of neighborhoods, Ebe tried to wave to Kevin, who was sitting on the curb outside of the tent city encampment. He was smoking a cigarette and reading a paperback book with a busted spine. Ebe knew him from Food Not Bombs and they and Marley had chained themselves to him in an anti-war protest, ten years ago...

"Where has all the time gone?" Ebe wondered to themself. The world felt as broken as it ever had, and what had they done? Written a paper... But what did they have to show for the commitment to the cause? Lots of questions, no answers, a lot of unmet desires, and an empty bed. HUMBUG.

The spirit continued to pull Ebe past tent city. Kevin, of course, didn't see them. The spirit pulling Ebe turned after the freeway overpass, down an alley, then out onto a small dark street. The city hadn't bothered to string Christmas lights along the lampposts of this avenue lined with bars, bad disco drifting from the windows of one. Another door opened and out poured glistening half naked cis men, and a beautiful woman in stiletto boots and blue twists, along with the sound of Christmas carols remixed into vogue beats. The last bar on the left flew rainbow, bear and leather flags. Ebe thought for a moment they were going in, but the spirit shook her head and pulled them down a flight of stairs to the left of the door into The London. As they descended, Ebe closed their eyes.

HUMBUG HUMBUG HUMBUG HUMBUG HUMBUG

Their head was so loud. The fear hadn't been this loud in so long. Ebe didn't know what to do. They wanted to run, but which direction? Up the stairs and back to their empty bed, or down the stairs into Daddy Freddie's arms?!

"Why is everything so complicated?" Ebe asked.

The spirt gave an infuriating smile and a little giggle before she pushed open the door. The dungeon was packed and at the center Ebe knew would be Freddie and Olivia. The dungeon was run by the bar, but Olivia helped Freddie with coordinating all of the scheduling of classes and play parties and special events—like, of course, the annual leather Christmas party.

The room was filled with the smells of cookies and hot chocolate. There was a black Christmas tree and a big leather bear in a red Santa suit partially unbuttoned revealing thick brown chest hair, bilateral scars and a silver nipple ring. The spirit drifted away to a table of littles coloring pictures of elves and Victorian carolers. The spirit sat herself on an empty chair. Ebe knew they couldn't avoid that corner, because in the middle of the crayons and the teddy bears was Olivia. She looked adorable in pigtails and a ruffly red dress with green stockings. The littles were coloring and playing a guessing game.

"My turn!" A little boy called out. Ebe didn't know this boy very well, but despite their capitalistic critique, Ebe thought the cartoon characters tattoo on his arms were really cute.

"Is it bigger than a breadbox?" Olivia asked.

"Yes," said the boy.

"Is it an animal?" asked a shy girl.

"Kinda," the boy replied.

"Is it... an elephant?"

"No."

"Do people want it around?"

"Not usually," replied the boy.

"Is it cute?" Olivia asked.

"You thought so," said the boy.

"Is it glitter?" Olivia said hesitantly. Ebe could tell that she was getting bored with this game.

"No sillyface —it's Ebe!"

"That's not nice!" Olivia yelled. But was that a smile on her face? Ebe wasn't sure.

"I really don't know what you and Freddie see in them," the boy continued. "They are cute but they aren't any fun, and besides they stood you up, on Christmas!"

Ebe was standing right next to Olivia and her friends, but of course there was no way they could have known that Ebe was there with the spirit, hearing these jokes. Ebe didn't know what to do. They wanted to leave the dungeon, to get as far away from this as they could.

Olivia's eyes filled with tears. Ebe felt so guilty. The last thing they wanted to do was to hurt Olivia, or Freddie. They were so sweet, so loving. They had opened up their home and created the possibility of bringing Ebe into the family, and again just like with Bee, Ebe had fucked everything up so much.

Olivia turned back to her little friend, wiping tears off her cheeks. "When my Daddy found me I was so much like Ebe. I didn't know how to accept kindness, I didn't know how to have a Daddy or be a good girl, or how to even dream of magic. I didn't know how to do any of these things and Daddy never gave up on me, hy saw something, something inside me that was worth fighting for. No, not really fighting, more like tending, growing, cultivating. Daddy saw me before I could fully see myself, or admit what I wanted. Daddy didn't give up on me, hy built this world for me, and I want to do the same for Ebe."

"Seems like it's been a lot of cat and mouse," the little boy responded.

"It has been, and if something doesn't change soon I'm not sure how much more Daddy and I can take. Christmas is sacred. We've been doing this shit with Ebe for a long time now and I am afraid my patience is almost gone, but I just don't want to give up yet. I don't know why, but I believe that something is going to change, that one of these days Ebe is going to fucking figure their shit out, and I want to be there to see that happen. Daddy likes a challenge, and I want to be a big sister to them, I want to help them. Did I tell you about the date to the pottery shop? It was fucking perfect. No, really! It was seriously everything that the three of us have talked about having together—and Ebe let themself go there!"

"Yeah, but then they stood you up," Olivia's friend responded.

"I know... Like I said, Daddy likes a challenge but I'm not sure how much more hy will put up with," Olivia sadly replied.

HUMBUG.

Ebe pressed their eyes closed and the world went black.

Part 4:
Reckoning

Ebe was done with flashbacks or nightmares or visions or whatever you wanted to call them. It was late when they woke again, sweaty and tangled in their black sheets. Ebe reached for their cell phone and thought about posting online about the night they were having, but thought someone might call the cops, thinking they were a danger to themself, if not others. Ebe wasn't so sure they weren't. This was the kind of stuff that could get you put on a 72-hour hold real easy. Ebe was pretty sure that it was all real and not delusions, which made the night even scarier. Their cell phone said it was 3am, so the final ghost should be arriving for them soon. Ebe thought of texting Freddie, asking hym to meet up at the bar for a drink at last call.

HUMBUG. It was Christmas Eve, Ebe remembered. Freddie would be home. Ebe thought of how sweet hy was to them and all the tender conversations they had about life and leather and compatibility. Freddie and Olivia were everything Ebe had ever wanted, if they could just let themself have it.

Ebe fell back asleep even though they didn't want to. They wanted to stay awake. They didn't think they could handle another vision, but yet they couldn't make themself stay up. It was like something was pulling them to blackness, pulling them into the deepest night. Ebe wished Marley would come back. They wished that in that moment they didn't have to be alone, and that they could be comforted by their closest friend. Ebe had chased hir out of the bedroom before, but at least Marley's spirit was familiar. They almost knew how to trust it.

Ebe started to drift off, but then—almost as though their window had opened—there was a burst of cold air. Ebe sat up. The window was closed, but there standing before them was a giant drag queen. She wore impossibly high platform heels, a black habit like a nun's, and dramatic makeup complete with red glitter lipstick and glitter in her goatee.

"So much to see! No time for lying about!" the drag queen boomed.

"W-h-o aaa-re you ?" Ebe stuttered.

"Oh darling, I am the spirit of Christmas yet to come. I promise you, sweet child, that the best is yet to come! You'll see, the spirit of the season will give you life!"

"Are you a nun?" Ebe asked, confused, not remembering the articles they'd read about the Sisters of Perpetual Indulgence in their undergraduate queer theory class.

"Hahaha!" the drag spirit's ghost echoied around Ebe's bedroom. "Yes, of course."

"Doesn't God hate you?" Ebe knew they were being cruel, but they were too confused to remember any manners.

"Oh sweet child, there is much to teach you and not much time to do it in! We only have tonight! And we have much to see."

Ebe shook. They weren't used to all these visitors, and they were uneasy of what might be coming. The window opened and the spirit stepped outside, her dress billowing around her.

Ebe wanted to go back to sleep. They wished they had sleeping pills in their bedside table like they used to. But there was nothing in the drawer and a very real spirit standing in front of them, waiting for Ebe to get up. Ebe had learned enough tonight to know the spirit wasn't just going to just go away if they pulled the blankets back over their head and tried to dissociate.

"HUMBUG! Please, please. I can't bear it. SAFEWORD! SAFEWORD!" Ebe cried out, but the spirit only laughed. She pushed them forward, out the window and into the darkness.

The spirit's long black lace habit pooled on the snow but didn't get wet. She wore a black nun's wimple and looked terrifying against the whiteness of the snow.

Ebe opened their eyes and found themself at The London again. The spirit pushed them through the open door into the dimly lit room. On the counter of the bar they saw a plain wooden box. Around them everyone was dressed in black, not unusual for a dungeon, but the mood felt different. At first the conversation was like a roar of bees swarming. Nothing made sense, just a buzz of words, none of which they could catch.

"Poor bastard," Ebe finally picked out.

"Please. They did this to themself."

"Still, it's too bad they died alone."

"They liked being alone."

"They refused company from anyone, so what did they expect? Of course they went alone in that old house."

Ebe looked up at the spirit, not even able to form the words to ask if what they thought was happening truly was. The spirit said nothing but nodded toward the bar. Ebe walked forward, across the sticky floor. On the bar Ebe looked down at the tiny box, nothing fancy, didn't even have an official plaque or anything, just a sticker adhered from the crematorium with their name.

Ebe felt their hands start shaking. "No, spirit, please... humbug...." they whispered, knowing there was no safewording out of this now. Around them the voices grew loud again. They still couldn't fully follow the conversation, just little words here and there; laughing, mocking, no sadness.

"We aren't done," the spirit said, her voice like asphalt. The spirit and Ebe drifted away from the dungeon and down the familiar streets of Ebe's neighborhood. They were relieved to be away from the voices of all the queers but it was scary being out in the world with a ghost. For a moment Ebe thought about what kind of post they could write on social media that would make any contextual sense. They reached for their pocket but their phone was still at home on the nightstand. Probably better, anyway. How could they write about something like this in 140 characters!?

"You don't. This is the kind of thing you don't tell anyone about if you don't want to find yourself at the psych ER of your local public hospital," Ebe reminded themself.

It didn't take long for Ebe to realize they were heading to their house. Ebe shivered, wondering what was happening with the collective. Surely someone there would lighten their mood.

"How about all this paper and stuff?" a blue haired punk Ebe vaguely recognized asked their roommate Charles.

"Just recycle it," Charles replied absently while sorting through what had been Ebe's record collection. Their work, all the hours, a lifetime they had spent in the basement putting those papers and zines together. And for what?

Ebe heard Marley's warning echoing in their brain: "You can't take your politics with you to the grave."

Ebe sank into the snow. Their flannel pajamas were quickly soaked and they began shivering. This wasn't what they wanted. All they had ever wanted was to make the world a better place, and they knew they had. Sometimes, when they got a reader letter, Ebe knew they had been able to make an impact, but maybe that wasn't enough. To get here, Ebe had thrown away the chance at love, the opportunity to connect. HUMBUG. This had to end.

If this future Christmas were to happen, Ebe realized not only would they be alone and dead, but their work would end with them. In the end it wouldn't matter. They thought about Marley's warnings. There is more to life than work. You can't take your politics with you when you die. Sitting in the snow, Ebe started to wonder: do you have the ability to change the way people remember you? What if it's all too late to change? What if they don't remember you at all, and your work is rotting in a landfill? What if they didn't even have the decency to recycle! Ebe's mind stung with questions.

The spirit reached down. The sharp tip of her nail scratched Ebe's wrist as she pulled them up out of the snow and through the front door, which had been left ajar. The house looked the same, just emptier without all their newspaper clippings and show posters hung everywhere. The spirit led Ebe down the hallway and to the back bedroom, Cratchet's room. Ebe wondered why they hadn't been outside, why they weren't stopping the collective from destroying everything the two of them had worked on. Ebe thought for sure they would care about the work, about the cause. Cratchet's door was closed, but holding the spirit's hand, Ebe drifted through it. Things looked much as they had in the previous vision, of Christmas present: desk, bed, chair…

A tiny Christmas tree lit with rainbow lights glittered in the window; stockings hung on the windowsill. The tree sat upon Cratchet's tiny table. Hung on the back of their chair, empty, was the baby sling that Tiny always rode in; the sling that kept him nestled into Cratchet's chest as they cooked, wrote, or wandered the neighborhood waiting for Tiny's wheelchair fundraiser to work. Ebe saw Cratchet out of the corner of their eye. They were curled up on the plaid comforter of their bed, clutching Tiny's little Christmas stocking. Their face buried in their knees, shoulders shaking. Licking their hands was a pudgy black pit bull with a white splotch over her face. Suddenly Ebe realized, Tiny was gone.

"Spirit, no!" Ebe whispered, even though by now they knew the rules. They knew Cratchet couldn't hear them. "Spirit, please say this isn't true, that *this* isn't what must happen, that this is the vision of a Christmas that *might* come, but not a guarantee of what *is* coming."

Ebe dropped to their knees. "Please spirit, please give me a chance to change the story, to be someone else. I can change, spirit, I know I can. I have paid attention, I have listened to your lessons, I've paid attention to everything! I can live with love and kindness in my heart. I promise will honor everything I've learned tonight in these visions of past, present, and future Christmas! I will stop closing myself off, I will listen to Olivia and Daddy Freddie, I will honor the spirit of Christmas, living generously and openly with joy. I will prioritize love and connection above my politics. Please spirit, please!"

Part 5:

The End Of It All

Ebe woke up and all the visions, and everything from the night before was so fresh. The hem of their pajama pants was even still wet. At first Ebe could hardly believe that morning had really come, but weak sunshine was streaming through their bedroom window. The house was quiet, and Ebe remembered most collective members were away and that Cratchet must still be asleep. Ebe pulled up the blinds in their bedroom window, long ago bent thanks to the cat of an old collective member. The freshly fallen snow was clean and fluffy. Everything looked new, even them as Ebe saw their hazy reflection in the glass. Ebe caught Marley's newsprint eye on a poster. They grabbed their phone from the nightstand. It had a low battery, and the calendar app on the lock screen said it was December 25th. After the night they had, Ebe couldn't believe they hadn't missed Christmas.

They texted Olivia.

> **Ebe:** 8:09am
> **Is it still Christmas?**

> **Olivia:** 8:11am
> Ebe! Merry Christmas! It's Christmas morning! Where have you been?!!

> **Ebe:** 8:11 am
> It's been a really long night, I don't even know how to explain it all, but I'm sorry, I'm sorry for everything. I want to see you, and Freddie.

Silence. It took five minutes for Oliva to reply. Olivia's phone was always in her hand, always. The delay was paralyzing. Finally, Ebe's phone chimed.

> **Olivia:** 8:16am
> I think we should talk about this in person. Want to come over?

> **Ebe:** 8:16am
> Okay

Downstairs, Ebe heard Cratchet in the kitchen starting to boil water for tea and the back door creaking open. Ebe heard Cratchet's quiet whispers, low and sweet, to Tiny. Instantly they felt guilty, knowing that the low tones were in part because of them, because Cratchet feared Ebe's judgements. Oh, what a mess they had made of so many things. HUMBUG. They would not let their guilt keep them from making things right, especially with someone who had actually put up with so much of their crap.

Ebe tugged a light pink dress from the floor of their closet on over their head, pulled on striped stockings and crept to the staircase. They rushed outside into the morning light. Ebe wanted to get to Freddie and Olivia, to put into practice everything the night had taught them, but there was something that had to happen first. Ebe raced down the block to the butcher on the corner, this new artisanal place that went into the neighborhood a couple of years ago. Ebe didn't eat meat so had never been inside before. There was a painting of a pig on the back wall with markings to note where different cuts of meat came from. They were totally grossed out by how hipster it was and just wanted to walk out, but this wasn't about them. This was about Tiny.

"Hi. I'd like to buy a bag of the best bones you have!" they said to the man behind the counter. He had a huge beard like the one their redneck uncle used to have.

"Bones?"

"Yes! It's a Christmas gift for a special little dog." Ebe smiled bigger than they had in a long time, and they felt their lipstick crack at the edges.

The butcher couldn't help but smile a little. He turned and walked to the back of the shop. Ebe looked around and noticed a Christmas tree stand across the street. The butcher returned with a bag of bones, Ebe paid him and hurried out the door. They stopped in at the coffee shop next door, buying a cup for themself—it had been a very long night—and a second cup which they carried across the street and put in the tattooed hand of the punk tree seller down from Vermont. Her hands were red with cold, her blonde hair dreaded in a way that was culturally appropriative peeked out from a stocking cap. The old Ebe, the Ebe of yesterday, would have delivered a lecture, would have snatched back the cup of coffee away or never given it at all, but instead Ebe smiled. It wasn't that the fucked up appropriation didn't matter, or wasn't worth addressing, but Ebe had learned more than just the literal meaning of Christmas. They were thinking about redemption, of second chances, of tolerance and patience. Unicorns know they weren't perfect, never had been, never would be, and there was so much they would need to atone for. It was continuing to sink in for Ebe just how much damage they had done in the name of proving just how radical they were.

Realizing they were standing there just grinning at the cold punk, Ebe looked around at the sidewalk forest, inhaling the scent of Christmas. "I'd like that tree." They pointed a chipped red nail at a squat bushy tree next to them. The punk, whose name Ebe learned was Gretchen, tried to just give the tree to them after the coffee, and since it was already Christmas morning, but Ebe refused. They handed Gretchen a crumpled twenty dollar bill and told her to keep the change. Ebe also pointed down the street to their house, and invited her to come over before she left town. The promise of a hot shower and some food sealed the deal for Gretchen.

Ebe laughed as they tried to make their way back down the block hugging the Christmas tree, the bag of bones held in their teeth.

"Here, let me help you," Gretchen called after them.

Ebe smiled. If this was what their new life was going to be like, they could live with this. No, they could actually really like this, Ebe thought to themself.

When they got to the house, Ebe tried to invite Gretchen in right away but she declined. "Gotta get back to the trees, maybe you aren't the only one who procrastinated on getting one!" Gretchen replied, turning to go.

"Thanks again and don't forget to come over tomorrow before you leave!" Ebe called after her.

As Ebe opened the door, they could see Cratchet standing in the doorway cradling Tiny in their arms. Tiny was wearing a festive green sweater and Cratchet a bathrobe. Tiny was looking up at Cratchet. "Merry Christmas, my small one," Ebe heard Cratchet say as they held Tiny up to the window that looked out onto the small backyard. "Look at all this snow! How lucky we are to have Christmas together, just you and me!"

Ebe jostled the tree into the house and closed the door. Cratchet turned and saw them standing, their bag of butcher bones in their mouth, and arms wrapped around the tree. Cratchet stood silently, just looking at Ebe with a confused look on their face. Tiny, in Cratchet's arms, spotted the bones dangling in the plastic bag from Ebe's red lips, and broke the awkward silence with the biggest bark he could muster!

Ebe and Cratchet both laughed.

"MERRY CHRISTMAS, TINY!!!" Ebe called out into the quiet house. "You've already spotted your present!" they continued, giggling.

Cratchet had never heard Ebe giggle. It was so sweet. "What is all this?" they asked. "Who are you and what the fuck have you done with my curmudgeon of a housemate?!"

Ebe swelled. They deserved that, and oh so much more.

"If I told you, there is no way you would ever believe me, but let's just say it's been a very long night, and this morning, it feels like everything is different. Can you ever forgive me for how I acted?"

Cratchet looked at them for a moment. Ebe swallowed nervously, worried they were going to press them to say more, that they were going to not be able to forgive them, or that they wouldn't want to. Ebe wouldn't have blamed them.

"Of course I forgive you," Cratchet whispered, "but I hope Freddie and Olivia can. That is, if your change of heart extends to them as well."

Ebe felt like their stomach was doing gymnastics. They forgot that Freddie and Cratchet were friends. Ebe wondered what they knew, and if everything was already ruined. With everything they had seen, Ebe realized how fucked up they had been about everything and they felt the panic starting to build. What if it really was too late to change things? Freddie and Olivia couldn't be won over with a bag of bones.

Ebe's panicked mind flashed to the vision the spirits had showed them of a Christmas yet to come, and the Christmas that was upon them now. The last spirit made them believe that change was possible, because if it wasn't then what would the point of the last night have been? HUMBUG HUMBUG HUMBUG.

Ebe's mind was spinning, but then they thought about how quickly Olivia had texted back telling them to hurry over for Christmas, that Santa had come but they hadn't yet opened presents!

"I hope I'm not too late," Ebe whispered. "I'm actually going to them now. Want to come with me?"

"Nice try, " Cratchet teased. "I'm pretty sure this is something you have to do on your own, besides it looks like Tiny and I have a Christmas tree to decorate!"

Tiny meanwhile was doing his best to open the bone bag. Cratchet turned to open it properly for him.

Ebe smiled. From their bag they pulled a thick manila envelope and left it on the table. They had drawn a Christmas tree on it with black sharpie and written "For Tiny" across the top. Inside the envelope was the $5,000 that they had saved up for the new computers and software. Ebe headed for the door, but before they got there Cratchet had turned around and saw the envelope on the counter.

"What's this?" they asked

"Just something for Tiny," Ebe replied, blushing and suddenly feeling incredibly awkward.

Cratchet peeled open the adhesive on the envelope and sat down when they peeked inside and saw all the cash.

"Ebe..." Cratchet trailed off. "This is the money for the new computers! This is the money you have been saving up for the paper!"

"And now it's for Tiny," Ebe replied.

"But..." Cratchet started.

"Look, the paper can survive another few years being laid out by hand, but what we can't live without is Tiny. He's family, and this is what family does. We have to look out for our own. I know that now."

Cratchet was crying and clutching Tiny in their arms while the small dog tried to wiggle back to his Christmas bones.

"I've done a lot of fucked up things, I know that now. I've justified the shit I've done by calling it activism, or saying it was about living my politics but I was a real dick. I want to figure out how to have balance now so that I don't let my politics keep me from supporting those who I love the most," Ebe finished.

"I don't know how I can ever thank you for everything that you've just done. Fuck... I..." Cratchet stammered.

"You don't have to thank me." Ebe smiled. "Just promise me something?"

"Anything."

"Promise that you will help me work differently. I'm not throwing all my politics away, I just want to try something new. I want to strive for balance and to do that I need to start thinking about more than just how to live my politics on the page of this paper, I need to be intersectional and I need to fucking make mistakes and have fun and..." They were spinning out on the enormity of what changing up their whole life would mean.

Cratchet saw that spiraling and thrust Tiny into Ebe's arms. Ebe held him and smiled.

"We got you," Cratchet whispered. "We will figure this all out together, but Christmas isn't a day for working, it's a time for family. I think you have other conversations to be had today. We will figure out the editorial vision of the paper tomorrow, or the day after. We've got time." Cratchet smiled.

Ebe handed Tiny back to Cratchet and headed back out onto the street. Ebe walked fast to the subway, stopping only to buy a wreath from Gretchen. The subway platform was filled with kids in Sunday finest, black patent leather shoes and small suits. Ebe felt a little out of place, and yesterday they would have scowled at all the fuss, at the irrelevance, the consumption apparent as adults held large shopping bags filled with wrapped packages. But today, today felt different. While Ebe tugged their pink hair into pigtails, they noticed the way the families laughed, tenderly holding hands and exchanging smiles, not just to each other but to them, and all the other strangers waiting on the platform. When the train came, everyone squeezed onto benches, clutching Tupperware with potluck dishes, or packages.

The sidewalks were slick as Ebe walked down side streets towards Freddie and Olivia's place. They were terrified. The panic had them starting to be convinced that Olivia's text invitation that morning was just a cruel joke—a way to get back at them for having disappeared, for having stood them up. Ebe rationally knew that was not how Olivia worked, and that it certainly would be behavior that Freddie would not encourage or even permit to occur under hys roof, and yet... Ebe worried. They didn't feel worthy of this, of a second chance, of love, of a Daddy, of a family... of any of it.

Ebe thought about Marley, how much they missed hir and how scary the vision of the night before had been. They thought too about the warning Marley had given them. How ze didn't want to see Ebe as alone as ze became. Ebe owed it to Marley to at least try, they thought as they reached Freddie and Olivia's building and made themself press the buzzer to their apartment.

Bzzzzzzzzzzzz. The door unlocked

Ebe wanted to linger in the stairwell, they wanted to turn and run, but they forced their feet up each step. Ebe didn't let themself pause on landings, refused to give themself the opportunity to change their mind, to run away. Ebe's old habits were so alluring, so easy, so comfortable, but they knew where those patterns led. That, if nothing else, had been made so clear after last night.

Ebe had never wished anyone lived in a higher walk-up, but on this morning they found themself wishing for more stairs. Spilling out from all the other apartments they passed on their climb were the sound of laughter, carols and the smells of cooking Christmas dinners.

Ebe stopped on a landing, laying their head against the cool wall. They watched a roach crawl into a hole and closed their eyes and tried to focus on breathing. HUMBUG. HUMBUG. HUMBUG. Everything in Ebe's head was racing, candy canes and collars, and ghosts and panic. Panic. Panic. Ebe wasn't sure if they'd ever been so afraid. There was no doubt the kind of life they wanted, the kind of relationship they wanted to have with a Daddy, and here it all was, right in front of them: the opportunity have it all, to have the kind of family they had dreamed of. Yet, the idea of throwing it all away was so easy, so alluring. It would be so easy to just walk down the stairs, to walk out of the building...

Ebe felt their purse vibrate, and pulled out their phone. There was a email blast from an activist group. They were doing a protest at a shopping mall tomorrow morning. They were protesting the disgusting nature of capitalism. The subject line of the email was:

"Santa is Capitalism's Wet Dream"

Ebe paused on a landing, skimming the email. Within the first paragraph the activists had managed to rally animal rights folks, since Santa's coat was traditionally trimmed in fur. They had probably pissed off some other activists since they were playing into the obesity epidemic, calling out Santa's size as a metaphor for greed... and then Ebe turned their phone off. They had never done such a thing before. On any other Christmas they would have been immediately writing the activists back, scouring their social media pages, finding ways to cover their protest. Ebe shoved their phone back in their purse and climbed the final set of stairs.

Ebe was just about to knock on the door, but at that moment Olivia swung it open! Ebe didn't know what to say—they thrust the huge Christmas wreath into Olivia's arms. Ebe's hands were sticky with sap and the whole landing was filled with the most intoxicating pine smell.

There wasn't time for Ebe to panic or to question what everything meant.

Everything was happening now, and if they wanted to avoid the fate they'd seen they had to get their anxiety under control. They had to live beyond the fear to do the hard work to have the life they wanted. Ebe followed Olivia inside.

The house was warm and glowing under the light of Christmas trees. There was one in the living room, and a small one on the little side table next to the door. There were carols playing. Ebe stalled in the entryway, while Olivia skipped ahead, then came bounding back towards them from the living room. Olivia was wearing red and green polka dot Christmas pajamas, with pigtails in her hair and reindeer slippers whose noses lit up red every time she walked! She was smiling and giggling, and grabbed Ebe by the hand before they could even think to resist and dragged them into the little living room.

The living room at Freddie and Olivia's place was a magical little place and this morning it felt even more so—filled with hope and chance—exuding possibility. There was of course the big Christmas tree in the corner, with packages underneath, and on the mantle perched their two big orange cats. Someone, Olivia most likely, had put green velvet ruffles with jingle bells sewed onto the collars around their necks. Under the cats were stockings with the cats' names embroidered onto them, Freddie's big green stocking, Olivia's little green stocking and…their hands flew to their mouth, a little one for Ebe too.

Next, Ebe's eyes turned to the tree. It was huge, real, the whole room smelled like forest. Under the tree there were piles of presents. Olivia ran, slippers sliding on the hardwood, over to the tree and picked up a little package and thrust it towards Ebe:

"This one is for you!"

Ebe was embarrassed, and they hated being embarrassed. Ebe's eyes filled with tears.

"But… I don't have anything for you, or Freddie," they responded. "All I brought was the wreath."

"THAT'S OK! Christmas isn't about getting presents! Christmas is about so much more than that! It's about family, the one we create, the traditions we make together. You being here is the best present I could get, and I know it's the best present that Daddy could get. You being here right now is giving us hope, and possibility of the family that we've always wanted to have with you."

Olivia set down the package and grabbed Ebe's hand. "We do have to talk, though. You really hurt us last night by disappearing. All of this only works if we can trust each other, and right now, I'm not sure if Daddy and I can trust you. Like, really really trust you," Oliva finished.

"Should I go?" Ebe asked, tears threatening to spill.

"I didn't say that," Olivia said, again handing Ebe the little wrapped box. Ebe opened the red and white striped wrapping paper and inside was the coffee cup they had painted on their last date.

Ebe was so overwhelmed they bit their lip, refusing to let themself turn and run. Their mind was racing, panic threatening to overtake them, but they fought it back. Ebe thought of Marley, of all the nights they had spent talking about Bee, about everything that Ebe had always pushed away and how they refused to let anyone in. Ebe thought about the first, second and third spirits, of all the lessons they had been taught, the importance of looking beyond capitalist failings, and the chance to build something beautiful, to build the kind of family that they had always wanted, to not be a prisoner of their own politics. Ebe shivered at the thought of what it would mean to walk out the door, and down the stairs, to again turn away from the possibility of being loved; to turn away from the possibility of being happy. HUMBUG.

At that moment Freddie walked out of the kitchen. Hy was standing in the doorway to the living room in plaid pajamas and a silly Santa hat, holding a plate of cookies.

Ebe tried to smile but started crying. They were embarrassed for so much.

"Merry Christmas, Sir. I am so sorry," they offered.

"Merry Christmas, little one," hy whispered.

Freddie and Olivia gestured to the comfortably worn couch and sat down. Ebe curled up between them. They were so afraid, so embarrassed, and yet they felt at home.

"I'm so glad to see you," Freddie started. "We were so worried, and hurt when you blew us off and disappeared."

The tears spilled from Ebe's eyes. "I know... I really messed everything up. I've been messing up for such a long time, but I want to be different. I want to change. I have already changed!" Ebe responded resolute and ashamed.

"In just one night? What could have changed since yesterday when you disappeared on us?" Freddie asked.

"Oh Daddy..." Ebe started. "I'm sorry. I probably don't have the right to use that word."

"Little one, we have grown to love you, we are just hurt right now. That doesn't mean we don't still want you. I just am trying to understand, trying to figure out how to trust that what you say is true, that overnight so much could have changed."

"Daddy, Olivia, I know it sounds stupid to say that I changed overnight. When people say that, they are usually just trying to take the easy way out but you wouldn't believe the night I had. Like really, if I told you what happened you wouldn't believe what I've seen..." Ebe trailed off. "I understand so much and I'm not who I was yesterday. I know that I have hurt you both, not just in the last couple of days, but I'm committed to doing the work I need to do in order to really change. I'm ready to be yours, to join this family. I don't have it all figured out, but I'm getting there, I know what's important, I understand I need to change. I want to prioritize building a family with you as something that can be compatible with my politics, and Tiny is going to be okay—I just talked to Cratchet and made sure of that—and I don't want to be lonely, and I know why Christmas is important, and I don't want to be alone, and I know I've been awful, and and and..." They stuttered, choking on tears.

Oliva squeezed Ebe's hand and Freddie grabbed the other.

"Slow down, sweet girl," Freddie whispered.

Ebe focused on their breathing. No need to safeword.

"Merry Christmas, little one, welcome home."

THE END

Acknowledgements:

This novella would not have been possible without the support from all of my queer and leather readers, especially those who connect with me on Facebook, Twitter, Instagram, and Fetlife. Thank you to my beta readers: Kestryl Cael Lowrey, Sophia Lanza-Weil and Emily Millay Haddad who provided early feedback. Thank you to Santa, Dasher, Dancer, Prancer, Vixen, Comet, Cupid, Donner, Blitzen and Rudoph for bringing Christmas to the houses of littles all over the world every year. Thank you to Michael Thomas Ford, and Laura Antoniou for your support of this project, and thanks to my little friends Jenni and Lola- your friendship and pen pal letters.

Thank you to MTA subway delays where much of this novella was written, my favorite bubble tea shop where I write on my lunch breaks, and the Saints & Sinners queer literary festival in New Orleans. Thanks to KD Diamond for the beautiful cover art, Jacob Tavares for the interior layout, and Gabrielle Harbowy for copyediting.

Most of all thank you to my Daddy for being my biggest supporter, for encouraging me to write this novella, reading and editing all my early drafts, building/encouraging my deep love of Christmas, and making every day we spend together magical .

Merry Christmas <3

Sassafras Lowrey is a straight-edge queer punk who grew up to become the 2013 winner of the Lambda Literary Emerging Writer Award. Hir books—*Kicked Out, Roving Pack,* and *Leather Ever After*—have been honored by organizations ranging from the National Leather Association to the American Library Association. Sassafras' latest novel *Lost Boi,* a queer retelling of Peter Pan, was released from Arsenal Pulp Press in 2015 and was a Lammy Finalist for Transgender Fiction. Sassafras lives and writes in Brooklyn with hir partner and five furry beasts. Learn more at www.SassafrasLowrey.com.